YUE
"DO YOU LIKE BIGGER ONES?"
ARIFURETA: FROM COMMONPLACE TO WORLD'S STRONGEST
ryo shirakome
takayaki
#2

SHEA

THE MASAKA INN

"SACRED STIGMATA OF LIGHT, DESCEND FROM THE HEAVENS AND SEAL MINE FOES—BINDING BLADES OF LIGHT!"
KAORI SHIRASAKI